Treasure at the Boot-fair

by Chris Powling

illustrated by Michael Reid

A & C Black • London

White Wolves Series Consultant: Sue Ellis,
Centre for Literacy in Primary Education

This book can be used in the White Wolves Guided Reading
programme with more experienced readers at Year 3 level.

First published 2004 by
A & C Black Publishers Ltd
37 Soho Square, London, W1D 3QZ

www.acblack.com

ISBN 0-7136-6839-3

A CIP catalogue for this book is available from the British Library.

A&C Black uses paper produced with elemental chlorine-free
pulp, harvested from managed sustained forests.

Printed and bound in Spain by G. Z. Printek, Bilbao.

Contents

For David and Sheila Hinton

Chapter One

Nobody likes a boot-fair in the rain. The customers don't like it because there aren't many stalls. The stall-holders don't like it because there aren't many customers. As for the mud and the wet – well, they get on everyone's nerves.

"So it's a good time for you to start, Cal," said old Mr Jessop. "It'll be easy helping me today."

“Boring, though,” Cal said.

“Boring, son? No, it won’t be boring. Boot-fairs are never boring, I promise you.”

Mr Jessop gave a huge, gap-toothed grin. His wobbly eye, the left one, jiggled madly up and down. “You think I’m a weirdo, don’t you,” he said, “what with these gaps and wobbles?”

"Not really," Cal fibbed.

"Well, *I* think I'm weird – weird as a widget more than likely. I must be, sitting here in weather like this."

The old man looked happy enough, though. He tilted his umbrella and peered hopefully at the sky. "Know anything about bric-a-brac, Cal?" he asked.

"Bric-a-brac?"

"Antiques, son – except not so posh."

Mr Jessop pointed at the fold-up table in front of him. The top of it was divided into boxes – dozens of boxes. Each box was cluttered with oddments. Cal glanced at them and pulled a face. "Looks like a lot of junk to me," he said.

"That's because you haven't read *The Handbook*."

"The handbook?" asked Cal.

"*The Bric-a-Brac Handbook*, son. You can't do without it at a boot-fair. Here, I've got a copy in my pocket."

Mr Jessop pulled something out of his raincoat.

It looked like a few photocopied pages stapled together. Yet his left eye still wobbled with excitement.

"Think of this as a map, Cal," he said. "A map that leads you to hidden treasure."

"Treasure?"

"Treasure!" said Mr Jessop, tapping his nose. "Mind you, the bigger the treasure, the more you've got to play fair with people. Know what I mean by playing fair, Cal?"

"Of course," Cal shrugged.

Already he was in a bad mood. Why was he doing this Saturday job? He was too young to be paid for it, after all. His mum had insisted he give it a try, though.

"You'll learn a lot from Mr Jessop," she'd said. "He's a very special kind of person."

"I can see *that*," Cal wanted to tell her. "For a start, he's as weird as a widget."

Chapter Two

By lunchtime, they hadn't had a single customer. "Reckon you can hold the fort for a while?" Mr Jessop asked. "Won't be long. Need to go for a Jimmy Riddle, that's all."

"A what?" Cal asked.

"You know …"

"Oh," said Cal. "That."

Mr Jessop tapped his nose again.

"If anyone should turn up while I'm away, son – well, watch out for hidden treasure. And play fair with them, okay?"

"Okay," said Cal.

No one would come, he told himself. Not with the rain as hard as ever. Probably he'd still be sitting here, reading *The Bric-a-Brac Handbook*, when Mr Jessop got back.

No such luck.

Mr Jessop was hardly out of sight when the girl arrived. She looked skimpy, somehow. Yes, that was the word for it – as if she might fade away at any moment.

She held something in her hand.

"Here," she said, in a skimpy-sounding voice. "How much for this?"

"What is it?"

"It's a wrist-watch."

"But it hasn't got a strap," Cal pointed out. "And it looks sort of old-fashioned."

"Like my granpa," said the girl.

"His watch, it was. I'm selling it for him. He's a bit short of cash at the moment. It'll really help him if you buy it."

Her lip was trembling as she said this. "It's a Rolex," she added. "Made of steel."

"Is it?" said Cal.

"Honestly, it is. Here, take a look. I really need to sell it. Twenty quid will do."

"That much?" Cal gasped.

"At least you can look, can't you?"

She sounded so near to tears, Cal couldn't refuse. He peered at the watch, closely. To his surprise, it *was* made of steel. The watch-face said "Rolex", too. Was it hidden treasure?

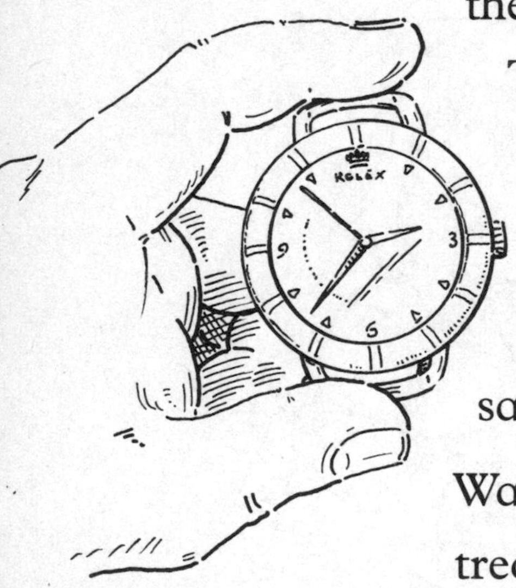

The girl hopped from one foot to the other like a small, skimpy bird. "Please," she begged. "It's for Granpa. It could be the last thing I ever sell for him."

"Really?" said Cal.

"Yes, really."

"Well …"

"Make it a tenner, then – okay?"

She was crying now. They were skimpy tears, it's true. But they were real tears, definitely.

Cal crossed his fingers behind his back.

"All right," he agreed. "A tenner it is."

His hand was shaking as he took the money from Mr Jessop's cash-box. Was an old watch really worth that much?

The girl stopped crying at once. She held the ten-pound note up to the light to check it wasn't a fake. "Cheers, kid!" she said when she was satisfied.

Cal could have sworn he heard her giggling as she hurried off into the rain.

Chapter Three

A real Rolex made of steel?

Cal had the sudden, sinking feeling he'd been tricked. Of course, he realised he should have checked *The Bric-a-Brac Handbook* before he gave her the money. Miserably, he picked up Mr Jessop's photocopy. As if to torment him, it fell open at the wristwatch section straightaway.

Cal let his eyes drift over the page.

Halfway down, he saw the Rolex. The picture was a little fuzzy but he recognised it at once. He lay the actual watch alongside it just to be sure.

"Hey …" he whispered.

Quickly, he read the words underneath.

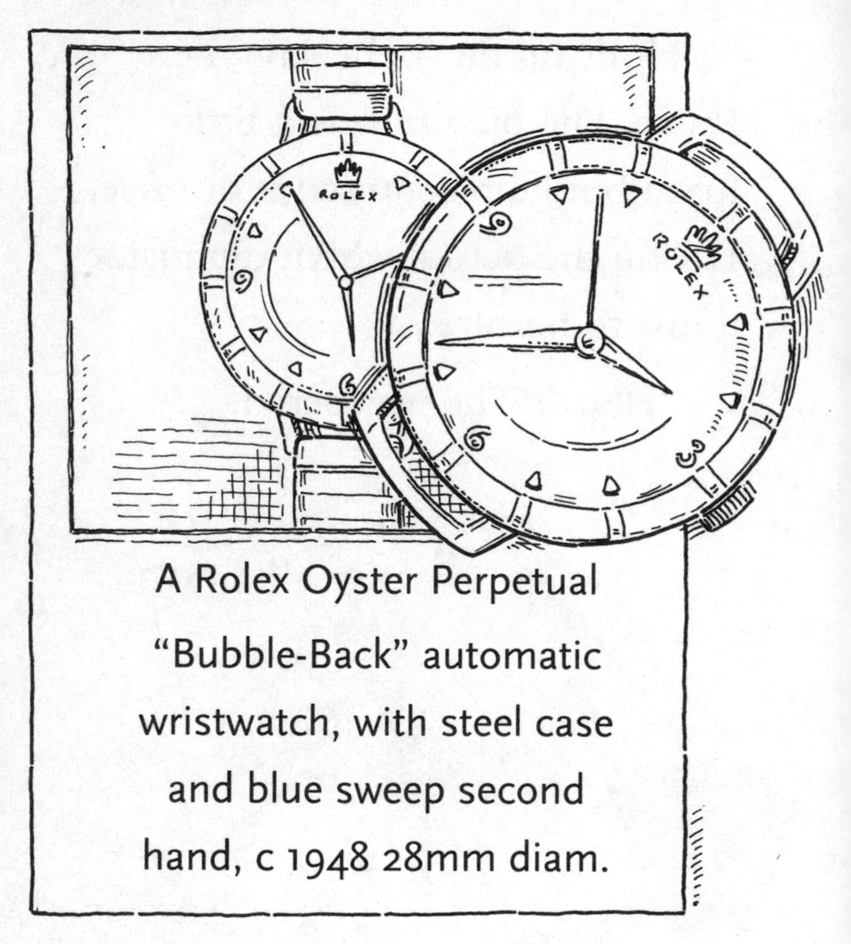

A Rolex Oyster Perpetual "Bubble-Back" automatic wristwatch, with steel case and blue sweep second hand, c 1948 28mm diam.

Everything fitted.

But that wasn't all. Below this, printed in bolder letters, it told you what the Rolex was worth. Cal heard his breath hiss through his teeth as he took the numbers in.

£1,000 – £1,200

He double-checked the details again.

Still everything fitted.

Somehow, he'd stumbled on hidden treasure with his very first customer! He'd made a profit of at least a thousand pounds. When Mr Jessop came back, he'd be thrilled to bits.

Or would he?

Suddenly, Cal remembered the old man's words. "Mind you, the bigger the treasure, the more you've got to play fair with people." That's what Mr Jessop had said.

Did that mean this girl and her granpa?

Chapter Four

Cal knew there was only one answer to his question. He must tell the girl everything. Could he still catch up with her, though?

A quick look at the Rolex told him she'd been gone five minutes already. If he waited for Mr Jessop she might disappear for ever.

Of course, he'd have to take all the oddments with him.

"They may look like junk to me," Cal sighed. "But what do I know? Every one of them might be hidden treasure!"

Luckily, the fold-up table had a lid which slotted neatly over the boxes. "Easy-peasy," said Cal as he clipped it into place. Except it wasn't so easy to carry with his feet slipping in the mud.

Especially hugging the cash-box as well.

"Off home, kid?" called another stall-holder. "Can't say I blame you on a day like this."

"Has a girl just passed here?" Cal asked. "A sort of skimpy girl with a smile on her face?"

"Looked like a puff of wind would blow her away?"

"That's the one!"

"You've just missed her. She went that way. Towards the bus stop out in the lane, I expect."

"The bus stop?" wailed Cal.

Panicking, he quickened his pace. That's what he tried to do, at least. Twice he fell headlong when he lost his grip on the fold-up table.

Once he dropped the cash-box – almost kicking it into a ditch as it hit the ground.

To his relief, when he finally skidded into the lane, the girl was still there. So was a bus, though. Her foot was already on the platform.

"Wait!" Cal howled. "Just wait a minute, can't you!"

"Who, me?"

"Yes, you!" Cal said.

The girl was staring at him over her shoulder. She already had a foot on the platform of the single-decker bus that snorted and rattled in the roadway.

Her eyes were suddenly wary. "What do you want?" she asked. "If it's your money back, you can forget it. Granpa really does need that tenner."

"It's his lucky day, then," said Cal.

"What?"

"This watch you sold me is really valuable!"

"Keep it, then. Granpa's got a new watch now. I gave it to him last birthday. That's only an old Rolex."

"I know it is," Cal said. "It was made in 1948. It's a Rolex Oyster 'bubble-back' worth more than a thousand pounds. Look, you can see for yourself if you like."

"Are you kidding me?"

She snatched the Rolex from his hand and stared at it, impressed. At that exact moment, the bus doors began to close. Hastily, the girl stepped on board before she was left behind. She was still gazing at the Rolex when the bus pulled away.

Chapter Five

Cal wasn't surprised Mr Jessop was waiting for him. There he sat, on his empty pitch, reading *The Bric-a-Brac Handbook*.

"Good to see you, son," he said, coldly. "Been somewhere nice?"

Cal bit his lip.

"Glad you've brought my stall back. Also my cash-box, I notice. Everything in order, is it?"

"Mr Jessop, I'm really sorry ..."

"About what, son?"

Mr Jessop's left eye wobbled, dangerously. Even his gap-toothed smile didn't seem quite so smiley now. Behind him, above the treetops, the sky was turning a brilliant blue.

The rest of the day would be wonderful, Cal realised. Pity he wouldn't be there to see it.

Awkwardly, he shifted from one foot to the other. "This girl came along to sell something," he began. "Just after you left me on my own, Mr Jessop. Skimpy-looking, she was."

"Go on, Cal."

Cal told him everything – about the watch, about her granpa needing money, about reading *The Bric-a-Brac Handbook* much too late.

"I took the table and the cash-box with me when I chased her," he said. "I didn't dare leave them behind."

Mr Jessop jerked a thumb at the battered Transit behind him. "Why not lock 'em in the van, son? The key was in the ignition."

"I didn't think of that," said Cal in dismay.

"What happened next, then?" said Mr Jessop.

"She was already getting on the bus when I caught her. I let her have another look at the Rolex. She still had it in her hand when the bus drove away."

"How about my tenner?"

"She took that with her as well," Cal groaned.

"I see," said Mr Jessop. "You call that playing fair, do you?"

Cal looked at him in surprise. The old man seemed to be laughing. Was he really a special kind of person? Or simply as weird as a widget?

"Son," he said, with a wink. "If you don't mind me saying so, I reckon it's time you put your brain in gear."

"What?"

"Just think about it a moment. A rare and pricey Rolex falls right in your lap ... on your very first morning just after I've left you alone. Does that strike you as *likely*, I wonder?"

"Likely?" said Cal.

Blankly, he stared at the old man. Then, suddenly, he understood.

"It was a set-up, wasn't it," he said. "You were both in it together, you and that girl."

"My grand-daughter, actually," said Mr Jessop. "Used to work with me on this stall.

Wants to be an actress one day. She checks out all my new helpers, you know – even if they are too young to be paid. Gives them a little test of character."

"And being a wally I fell for it!"

"A wally, son? Not in my book, Cal." Mr Jessop shook his head.

"You spotted the treasure, didn't you – eventually. And you certainly tried to play fair. Now, I'd call that a result. A pretty good result, in fact. So how do you fancy helping me on a permanent basis?"

"Every Saturday, you mean?"

"Week in and week out," said the old man.

Cal thought about it a moment. He thought about the Rolex and *The Bric-a-Brac Handbook*. He thought about playing fair with people.

He thought how pleased his Mum would be. So it didn't take long to decide. "Thanks, Mr Jessop," he grinned. "I'll stay and help this afternoon if you like."

"Suits me, son," said Mr Jessop. "Who knows, one day when you're a bit older, I might even start paying you!"

About the Author

Chris Powling was a teacher and headteacher for twenty years, and has also been the editor of the children's books magazine, *Books for Keeps*. Chris started writing his own books twenty-five years ago. Now he spends his time writing, talking about books to adults and children, and reviewing books on radio.

Chris is married with two grown-up daughters, and lives in South-East London.

Detective Dan • Vivian French

Buffalo Bert, the Cowboy Grandad • Michaela Morgan

Treasure at the Boot-fair • Chris Powling

Hugo and the Long Red Arm • Rachel Anderson

Live the Dream! • Jenny Oldfield

Swan Boy • Diana Hendry

For older readers ...

The Path of Finn McCool • Sally Prue

The Barber's Clever Wife • Narinder Dhami

Taliesin • Maggie Pearson

Shock Forest and Other Stories • Margaret Mahy

Sky Ship and Other Stories • Geraldine McCaughrean

Snow Horse and Other Stories • Joan Aiken